An Unusual Friend

Written by Michael Pellico

Illustrated by Christina Berry

See more children's books by Moonbow Publishing's at:
https://MoonbowPublishing.com

First Print Edition
ISBN 978-1-7339130-1-0
Library of Congress Control Number: 2019918377
Printed in USA

This book is dedicated to:
Sabrina Pellico
The inspiration for this story...
and many others.

And to my mother:
Helen Pellico
My hero and guiding light
throughout my life.

Sabrina and her brother Stephen spent
the evening inside reading in their thatched
roof home on a beautiful island in the South
Pacific. Outside a powerful storm was blowing.

1

Palm trees were bending over from the strong winds. They could hear the sound of giant waves crashing on the beach. It was a world away from their first home in the United States. Their parents were marine scientists and their family relocated so they could conduct their research.

Stephen and Sabrina quickly adjusted to island life, but had not made any new friends yet, as school was still several months away. They spent a lot of time with each other, exploring new surroundings.

"Better not go outside or a coconut could drop on your head!" Stephen tells his sister.

"Ha! That must be what happened to you!" She teased. Stephen replied with a silly face.

All night the storm raged but by morning, it had moved on, revealing a brilliant pink sunrise.

"Come on! Hurry and get dressed!" Sabrina shakes her still sleeping brother. "The giant waves must have swept up the biggest and most beautiful shells!" The two headed out to explore another day in paradise.

Their morning stroll takes them further down the beach. Approaching a large tide pool, Sabrina suddenly stops.

"Look! What is that in the water?" They look closer. "It's a baby shark!!!" they both say at once.

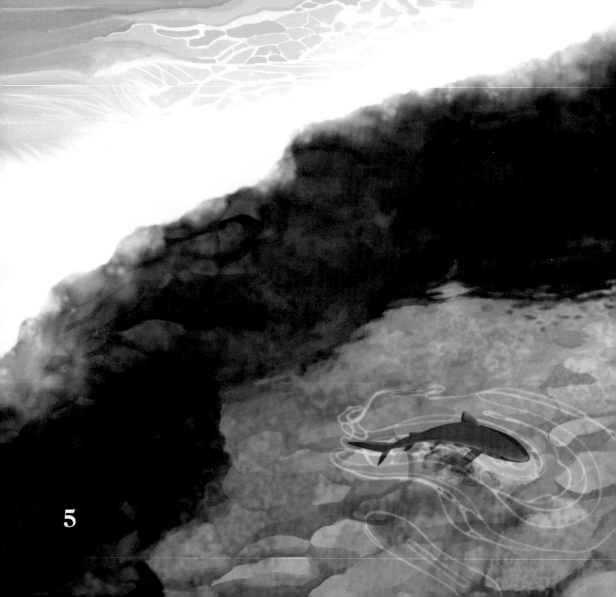

"Is it alive?" Stephen asked. "Yes its gills are moving water, but he's injured. "See the blood in the water?" replied Sabrina. "I think the storm must have washed him into the tide pool and cut him in the process."

"Wow! He is lucky to be in this tide pool, otherwise a bigger shark might smell the blood and find him."

"Yes, but now he is stranded..." Sabrina examined the shark from the rocks they stood on. "Look there, the blood is coming from the cut on his right pectoral fin."

"How can we help him? Mom and dad are on a diving trip," said Stephen.

"I know where they keep the waterproof bandages, let's go! It's up to us to help him!"

When they returned, Sabrina got into the water and carefully approached the little shark. She pet him until she felt comfortable putting her hands on its rough skinned body and flipping him upside down. She had learned from reading her parents' books that when a shark is upside down it stays completely still, almost like it was asleep. They let the wound air dry before securely wrapping it in waterproof bandage.

"It feels secure, but he cannot go in the ocean until it fully heals. The strong waves will pull the bandage off," said Sabrina.

"We can bring him food every day until he is better," said Stephen. Sabrina nodded in agreement. "He must be hungry now, let's see

if the fishermen have any small fish or shrimp they can give us."

So everyday Stephen and Sabrina brought the little shark shrimp and small crabs and fish. And everyday, the little shark was excited to see them, splashing about as they approached.

After two months, the shark's fin healed and he grew quickly in size. Sabrina and Stephen knew they would have to return him to the open ocean before he was too large to carry. By this time, the level of trust had grown so strong that the little shark remained perfectly still as the kids lifted him out of the water and walked towards the beach. Just past the shore break, they released him. Although he was free to swim away, the shark stayed.

"Look! He will not leave us." The little
shark kept swimming back and forth between
Stephen and his sister. "He wants to play some
more!"

When they got out of the water to go home, they were both quiet, thinking to themselves if this would be the last time they'd see their unusual friend.

The next day, the kids were overjoyed to see a dorsal fin in the water near the place they had left him. "Look!! There he is waiting for us!!"

They played for hours in the waves, where there were brand new places for them to explore together.

From then on Stephen and Sabrina went to play with the shark every day that summer until they had to go back to school. As the shark grew up, he could withstand colder waters and his appetite for larger prey drew

him further and further away from the beach. The unlikely friends did not see each other for some time, until one day...

Stephen and Sabrina were walking home from school when they saw a tourist boat going by. It made Sabrina nervous. "That boat is going too fast.

Even though the water is deep, there is a coral forest they are about to run into." Just as Sabrina finished saying this, the tour boat suddenly shuddered and there was a loud noise! The children gasped.

The coral caused major damage to the boat and it was sinking fast. People were screaming and jumping into the water. "What should we do?!" Stephen asked his sister.

"Let's take our boat out to retrieve them, I'm worried the impact may have injured some people and it would take us too much time to get help from adults."

Sabrina controlled the motor of their little boat as Stephen got the rope ready to lasso out to the flailing tourists in the water.

17

19

"Oh no!" Stephen yelled as they got closer. "Sharks are approaching! They can sense distress signals in the water from the people splashing!" They bravely decided to keep going.

As they neared the passengers, Sabrina shut the motor off and Stephen readied his lasso. Suddenly, they were thrown into the air and their boat was flipped over by a large shark that had slammed into its side. Stunned by the cold water, Sabrina and Stephen tried to climb onto their upside down boat. It was too slippery to get a firm grasp! As the sharks circled below their feet, they became very afraid...

Just then, with a thunderous rushing sound of water, a great white shark breached and the large shark that was headed straight for them was lifted out of the water in its jaws. With a shake of its powerful teeth, he tossed the shark far. And the rest of sharks swam away in fear.

"That is a Great White Shark! Now they are in bigger trouble!" the people shouted. But Sabrina and Stephen were not scared. They recognized him immediately by the scar on his right pectoral fin. "That shark is our friend," said Sabrina grinning. "He remembers us!" exclaims Stephen. The people looked on in disbelief. "I've never seen a shark behave that way before!" one said.

Sabrina took a deep breath and got face
to face with her old friend that she and her
brother had once found stranded in a tide pool.
Now as an enormous adult, he had come back
to save them.

23

24

What was a terrifying afternoon had turned
into a great adventure as they rode back to
shore on the back of their shark, towing the
people behind them to safety.

25

On the beach, the people rushed inland for help, but Sabrina and Stephen stood by the water as the sun set over the ocean. They waved goodbye to their unusual friend, unsure of when they would see him next, but confident they would meet again someday.

The End

About the Author

Michael Pellico is a medical researcher, writer, and film producer. One of eleven children whose parents both worked long hours. It was his responsibility to help raise his siblings. Growing up "poor", he entertained them with stories, and later telling stories to their children. This book and all his stories are dedicated to Sabrina, his niece, who insists that he tell her a story each time they are together. We hope that you love them as much as Sabrina does!

About the Illustrator

Christina Berry is an established book artist who enjoys all types of mediums in illustration. She has spent much of her adult life pursuing a degree in Microbiology and working with special needs kids, but she changed course to her first love; art. Christina works from home in Los Angeles, California and loves to foster and rescue cats.